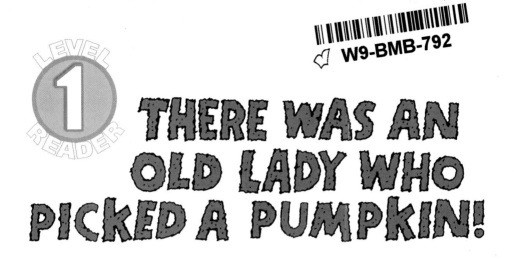

THERE WAS AN OLD LADY WHO PICKED A PUMPKIN!

by Lucille Colandro
Illustrated by Jared Lee

Scholastic Inc.

For Charlie, Hudson, Cooper, Olivia,
Matthew, Linus, Lucie, and Henry.
– L.C.

To Julie Ziegler Henschen.
– J.L.

Text copyright © 2023 by Lucille Colandro.
Illustrations copyright © 2023 by Jared D. Lee Studios.

ISBN 978-1-338-88295-7

10 9 8 7 6 5 4 3 2 1   23 24 25 26 27

Printed in the U.S.A. 40
First edition, July 2023
Book design by Doan Buu and Dave Neuhaus

The old lady says, "Hooray!"
We have a trip today!

3

Grab your bag. Say hello!
Get on the bus. Off we go!

Drive out of town. It won't be long.
Talk to friends and sing a song.

We see leaves all brown and red.
Who can guess what is ahead?

The old lady sees the sign.
Get off the bus. Step in line.

PUMPKIN PATCH

9

A friendly scarecrow points the way.
It's sure to be a fun fall day.

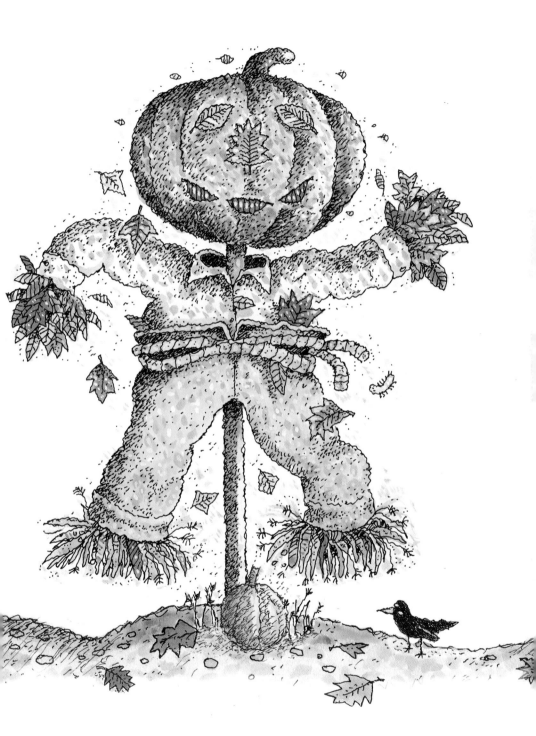

What does the old lady see?
A horse, a cow, and an apple tree.

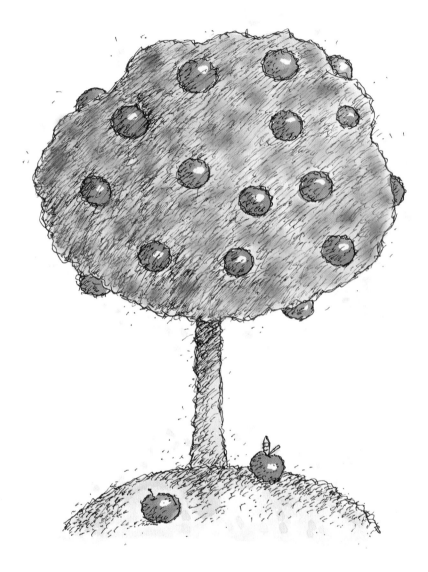

But no pumpkins!

Go up the hill. What does she see?
A field of hay and a bumblebee.

But no pumpkins!

See the lamb, the pigs, and the ducks.
They are on the big red truck.

But no pumpkins!

Look, look! What have we found?
Orange circles, nice and round.

Pumpkins!

No two pumpkins are alike.
Pick the one that you like!

Large, bumpy, small, or long.
Lift it up and take along!

Bye to pigs and lamb and ducks.
Bye to horse and big red truck.

Bye to cow. Bye to all!

See you next year. Happy fall!

Back to the bus for a ride.
Pumpkins are piled high inside.

Paint or carve? It's up to you!

The old lady knows what to do!

Yum!